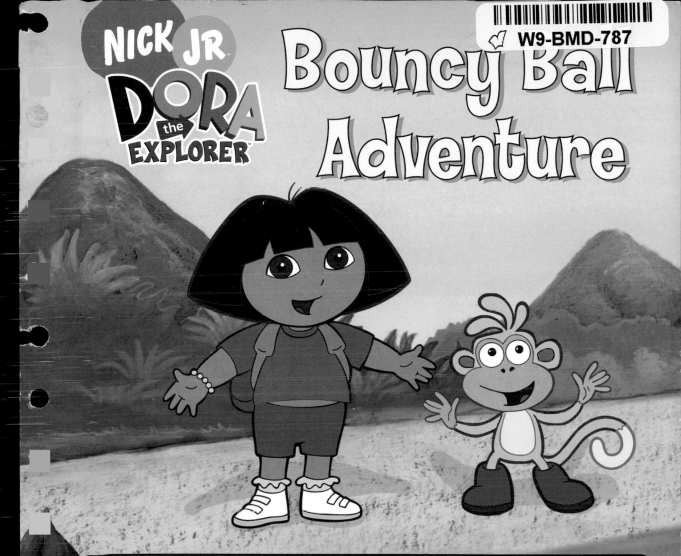

NICK JR
DORA the EXPLORER

Bouncy Ball Adventure

¡Hola! Boots and I are going on an adventure to Bouncy Ball Volcano. Will you read along and help us get there? Turn the page when you hear this sound.... When you finish reading the story, you'll find games to explore. Are you ready? *¡Vámonos!*

publications international, ltd.

¡Hola! I'm Dora and this is my best friend, Boots. Today we're playing with my baby brother and sister. They love to play ball! We have to watch out for that sneaky fox, Swiper! He'll try to swipe the balls. If you see Swiper, say, "Swiper!"

Oh, no! Swiper swiped the twins' bouncy balls.
We need to get them back for my baby brother and sister!

Where did the balls go? Let's ask Map!

Map says the balls bounced into Bouncy Ball Volcano.
We have to go through Spooky Forest and down Windy River
to get to Bouncy Ball Volcano.

Papi will look after the twins while we go find the balls.
Come on! *¡Vámonos!*

We made it to Spooky Forest! Aw, look! There's a lost baby bear cub! He can't find his *mami*! We need to help the baby bear cub.

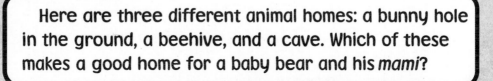

Here are three different animal homes: a bunny hole in the ground, a beehive, and a cave. Which of these makes a good home for a baby bear and his *mami*?

¡Sí! The baby bear cub lives in the cave. A hole in the ground and a beehive are too small for a bear cub and his *mami*.

Look—there's the baby bear cub's *mami*! She's so happy to have her baby back home. Thanks for helping!

Now that the baby bear cub is safe at home, we can keep going on our way to get the bouncy balls back! Where do we go next? *¡Sí!* The Windy River! *¡Vámonos!* Let's go!

We made it to Windy River! *¡Excelente!* But what can we use to go down the river?

¡Sí! The boat! We can use the boat to go down Windy River! But first, we'll need life jackets. Will you check Backpack for two life jackets for Boots and me?

¡Gracias! Thanks! Now that we're wearing our life jackets, we can go down Windy River!

There are so many rocks and turtles in the river! We need to paddle around the rocks! And we need to tell the turtles to watch out so they don't get hit with the paddles! The turtles speak Spanish, so let's tell them to watch out in Spanish. Say, "*¡Cuidado!*" Say it again with me! *¡Cuidado!*

Now that the turtles are out of the way, we can keep going down the river! Let's go!

We made it down Windy River! So now where do we need to go? Yeah, we need to go to Bouncy Ball Volcano to get the twins' bouncy balls back. But which road leads to the volcano? Road one, two, or three?

¡Sí! Road three will take us to Bouncy Ball Volcano. Thanks for helping!

We made it to Bouncy Ball Volcano! There are so many balls here. How are we going to find the balls that belong to my baby brother and sister?

Hmm. The twins' balls have stripes on them. We need to dig through the pile of balls until we find the two striped ones.

Let's jump into the pile on the count of three! One, two, three!

Now we have to dig through all the balls! Do you see any balls with stripes on them?

We did it! *¡Lo hicimos!* We found the balls! Now we can give them back to my baby brother and sister.

They're so glad to have the balls back. Thanks for all your help today. We couldn't have done it without you! *¡Gracias!*

Paddle Away!

Number Hunt!

Count with Me!